Read by myself

Kangaroo Daniel and the Runaway Pony

DILYS GOWER

SCRIPTURE UNION

130 CITY ROAD LONDON EC1V 2NJ

© Dilys Gower 1994
First published 1995

ISBN 0 86201 965 6

British Library Cataloguing-in-Publication Data.
A catalogue record for this book is available from the British Library.

Phototypeset by Intype, London.
Printed and bound in Great Britain by Cox & Wyman Ltd, Reading.

Kangaroo Daniel and
the Runaway Pony

Chapter 1

Ashley pressed his nose against the car window. Outside, everything he could see was green. There were green fields, green hedges, and green trees. Beside him on the back seat of the car, Daniel, his friend, was wriggling around. His elbows were digging into Ashley's side. Daniel was always wriggly and bouncy. That was how he had got his nickname, 'Kangaroo Daniel'. One of his teachers had said he bounced around the classroom like a kangaroo, and the name had stuck.

Ashley had once found Kangaroo Daniel really hard to get on with, but now they were good friends. They were going together to stay for a week with Ashley's Aunt Beth. She lived a long way from their home, right out in the country.

Daniel leant forward so he could see Ashley's mum in the driving seat of the car.

'Are we nearly there yet?' he asked, for about the tenth time.

'Daniel, you asked me that seconds ago,' said Ashley's mum. 'And the answer's the same. I don't know. This is the first time I've been to Aunt Beth's new house. But I don't think it's far now.'

'It's going to be a great week,' said Daniel. 'I hope it's as good as last time!'

When they had been on holiday together before on a canal boat, Ashley and Daniel had really become friends. They had done a lot of things together since then. They played in the same football club. They went to the same swimming group and to the same church. They were in the same class at school. In the week, Ashley's mum collected Daniel from school. And every Friday he went round to Daniel's house, where Daniel's mum always let them choose what to have for supper. Sometimes she let them help her cook it! Today, they even looked the same. They were both wearing new black T-shirts, with stars and planets on them. Daniel's mum had bought them as a 'going-on-holiday' present.

Ashley's mum turned the car off into a narrow lane. 'I think Aunt Beth's is somewhere down here,' she said. 'Not far now. She said there was a farm, and the lane got very narrow. Hers is the end bungalow.'

Ashley wrinkled up his nose. 'This lane's really muddy,' he said, 'and smell that!'

His mum laughed.

'You're in the country now,' she said. 'Things are different. There will be more cows than cars using the lane. That's why it's muddy. And the smell is from the farmer's silage store.'

'What's a silage store?' asked Daniel. But he never found out because just then Ashley's mum stopped the car outside a small bungalow, with a neat grass front garden. Kangaroo Daniel jumped out of the car, banging the door behind him. The front door of the bungalow opened and out came a tall woman in jeans, with long hair tied back in a ponytail.

'She doesn't look like an aunt,' whispered Daniel loudly.

Aunt Beth looked at him and smiled. She helped Ashley's mum get all the bags and stuff out of the car. Then they went into her little sitting room and the boys were given a glass of lemonade and a big plate of biscuits. The room was very tidy. There were no heaps of newspapers and no toys. And even worse, there was no television.

'What are we going to do all week?' Daniel whispered to Ashley. 'There isn't a television.'

His whisper wasn't quiet enough and Aunt Beth heard him.

'It's a long time since I've had anything to do with boys their age,' she said to Ashley's mum. 'I hope they won't be bored here.'

'I'm sure they'll be fine,' she answered cheerfully. 'They usually are. Perhaps they could go and unpack, while you and I catch up a bit.'

Daniel put his glass down on the table, missing the mat which had been put out for it. The glass left a wet circle on the table and Aunt Beth dabbed at it with a tissue.

'You're sharing the back bedroom,' was all she said. 'I hope you like it.'

Ashley and Daniel unpacked quickly by tipping their things into the empty chest of drawers. They knelt on one of the beds to look out of the window. It felt strange to be in a bedroom downstairs, with the garden on the same level as them. The garden was small, and as neat as the sitting room, with a tall fence going right round it.

'I don't know if I'm going to like it here,' said Daniel. 'There doesn't seem to be much to do. And your Aunt Beth's a bit fussy.'

'I think she's all right,' said Ashley. 'She's quite smiley. Let's go out into the garden. There might be something really exciting the other side of that fence.'

'Oh yeah,' said Daniel, 'like fields you mean!'

He got up and followed Ashley out into the small garden.

Chapter 2

The garden seemed even smaller when they were out in it. It was a square shape, with the big fence going all the way round. There was a patch of grass in the middle, and square flower beds in each corner. The path round the edge was made of a pattern of bricks. The flower beds were full of brightly coloured flowers, each one planted in its own space, with a circle of earth around it.

'It's quite pretty,' said Ashley.

'I think it's boring,' said Daniel. He bent down and picked up one of the flowers, pulling off the yellow petals one by one, and letting them drop on the path as he walked.

'There's no room for football. There's nowhere to make a den. There are no trees to climb. All we can do is go round and round this path.'

He began to jog slowly and then got faster and faster until he was running round the brick path in a tight circle.

'It's a running track,' he shouted. 'I'm in front. I'm winning.' He ran even faster, pumping his arms up and down at his sides. 'I'm

winning, I'm winning. I've won!'

He stopped running and started jumping up and down, punching the air with his fists.

Ashley laughed.

'Let's see what's the other side of the fence,' he said.

The fence was too high for them to see over, even on tiptoe. They looked around for something to climb on, but in that tidy garden there wasn't much to choose from. They saw a sweeping brush, a wheelbarrow and a watering can. Daniel chose the wheelbarrow. He wheeled it over to the end fence and propped it up.

'Hold it still,' he said to Ashley, 'and I'll see if I'm tall enough if I climb on that.'

Despite Ashley's grasp, the wheelbarrow wobbled as he climbed up. He found he could hold the top of the fence with his hands, but he still couldn't see over.

'We'll have to try something else,' he said.

As he was getting down, Ashley's mum called from the house.

'Ashley, I'm going. Come and say goodbye.'

'You go,' said Daniel. 'I'll stay here and see what I can do.'

Ashley stood in the tiny hall and hugged his mum. Now that the time had come for her to go, he didn't want her to leave.

'I'll miss you,' he whispered.

'And I'll miss you too,' whispered his mum. 'You are very special. But you've got Aunt Beth here and Daniel. Even better, God is here, because he promises to be with us all the time.'

'I want you to stay,' said Ashley quietly.

His mum gave him an extra large hug. 'The

week will go very quickly. I don't suppose you'll want to leave at the end of it. I'll think about you every day. Now be good for Aunt Beth, and do what she says. One more hug.'

Ashley hugged her so tightly that his arms felt weak afterwards. He tried to wave bravely as she got in the car, and turned round in the narrow lane. She pressed the horn loudly as she drove away.

'Enough to make the cows jump over the hedge in fright,' said Aunt Beth. 'Pop back into the garden with Daniel, Ashley, and I'll get us something for supper.'

Ashley walked slowly round to the back garden. Kangaroo Daniel was standing on the side of the watering can, which he had put on top of the wheelbarrow. His hands were round the edge of the fence, his knuckles white from holding on so tightly. There was a long scratch down the side of his leg.

'I slipped the first time,' he said, seeing Ashley looking at his leg, 'but it's brilliant. Guess.'

Ashley looked up at the high fence. He was

still feeling a bit sad because his mum had gone, and wasn't sure he wanted to play guessing games with Daniel.

'A supermarket,' he said, half-heartedly, 'or a car park?'

'Don't be silly,' said Daniel crossly. 'We are in the country after all.'

'All right then,' said Ashley, 'give me a clue.'

'They make noises and you can fall off.'

'A motor-bike track,' said Ashley, brightening up, 'or a skateboard park?'

'You're not trying,' said Daniel. 'We're in the country.'

'All right,' said Ashley, 'I give up.'

He put his foot onto the wheelbarrow and his hands round Daniel's waist. Everything wobbled, but Ashley managed to get the other foot onto the watering can and pull himself up so he could see over the fence.

He looked over.

'It's horses,' he said in a disappointed voice. 'What's so good about horses? I don't like them.'

'I think it's a riding school,' said Daniel.

'Look!'

The other side of Aunt Beth's fence there was a wide strip of grass. Then there was a low fence, and then a big sandy patch of ground, with a wooden rail going all the way round it. On the far side of the rail they could see white letters painted, A. K. E. H. C.

'I wonder what that spells?' said Ashley. 'Perhaps there are some more letters on the side we can't see.'

Daniel didn't answer. He was watching as a horse and rider came out from some wooden buildings, and went over to the sandy patch. The rider bent down to open the gate. Ashley could see she was a girl, older than he was. She had a long, gingery-coloured ponytail hanging down her back, under her riding hat. She was sitting very straight and still on the horse, and she had a long stick in her hand. The horse was black and had a sort of red cloth under the saddle.

'I told you,' said Ashley. 'I don't like horses.

'No, watch!' said Daniel. 'This is good.'

The girl was riding her horse in a wide circle on the sand, slowly at first, and then she changed into a fast, flowing movement. She turned across the area and went over a jump which was set in the middle, bending forward as her horse rose over it.

'Look at that,' said Daniel. 'I wish I could do it.'

'It looks easy,' said Ashley. 'I can't see anything clever about it.'

'We could ask Aunt Beth if we could go over,' Daniel said eagerly. 'I'd really like to have a go.'

Ashley didn't answer. He had looked away from the girl, towards the wooden buildings. It looked quite busy. There were several horses standing about, tied up, while people worked around them. He could see a brown and white one, another black one, and a funny beige coloured one. A girl near that one seemed to be squirting water onto its legs from a hose. The horse was standing quite still.

He saw a man wheeling a barrow into one of the sheds. Then a small tractor with a trailer behind it drove into the middle of the yard.

Now that looks more fun, he thought to himself, a tractor.

'OK,' he said out loud to Daniel, 'we'll ask Aunt Beth if we can go round.'

Chapter 3

Aunt Beth was a friend of Dave Samuels, the man who owned the stables. She was pleased that Ashley and Daniel had thought of something they wanted to do and phoned him up first thing the next morning.

'He'll be very pleased to have you,' she reported back. 'You can go over by yourselves. It's not far. The way in is just past the other houses up the lane. He said you could stay as long as you liked, and he'd show you around.'

'That's great, Aunt Beth,' Ashley said, giving her the sort of bear hug he usually kept for his mother.

It was a lovely morning, sunny and warm. When they got there, they saw Mr. Samuels standing in the middle of the yard.

'You can call me Dave,' he said. 'Everyone else does. Nice lady, your aunt. Glad to have you kids here. Not too busy this morning, so I'll show you all round. No running off though. Stables are dangerous places. You must do as you're told.'

Ashley and Daniel nodded. There was something about this large, cheerful man that made them certain they would do as they were told.

And Ashley knew he didn't feel much like running off. Although he wouldn't have said so to anyone, and especially to Daniel, he was feeling just a little bit scared. Up close the horses were so big. Their hooves clattered noisily on the hard surfaces as they moved around. And he didn't much like the way they wrinkled up their lips to show heavy, yellowed teeth.

He watched quietly as the ginger-haired girl put a saddle on the back of one horse which was tied up near them.

'He's called Napoleon,' said Dave. 'A lot of our men riders use him, because he's big and strong.'

'What's she doing?' asked Daniel.

The girl was reaching up, joining the buckles on a leather strap which went round Napoleon's head.

His ears were twitching backwards and forwards as she worked.

'She's putting his bridle on,' said Dave. 'He doesn't like people fiddling round his head.'

Ashley watched as the girl pressed her thumb into the side of the horse's mouth. The horse opened its mouth and she slid the bit, the metal bar of the bridle, right into it.

Dave saw the look on Ashley's face.

'He won't bite,' he said. 'Horses have a place without teeth just there. Sometimes, if they won't open their mouths straight away you can make them do it by pressing your thumb in that gap there.'

I wouldn't put my fingers into a horse's mouth, thought Ashley to himself. I think she's brave.

'You must meet Vicky,' said Dave. 'She's a bit older than you. Her dad's a friend of mine. She's been helping down here since she was quite small. She knows what she's doing around horses by now.'

Ashley and Daniel looked at Vicky as she led the big horse past them. She looked back at them, but didn't smile.

'Can we see the other horses?' Daniel asked eagerly. 'Where do you keep them all? What do they eat? And what about the tractor? Can we go on it?'

Dave laughed. 'One thing at a time,' he said. 'We'll start over here.'

Dave took them round the rows of stables. Each stable had its floor covered with a deep layer of straw. Each one had a bucket of water in the corner, standing in an old tyre so it wouldn't tip over, and a net of hay hanging from the wall. Some were empty, and in others a horse was standing patiently, lifting its head to look at them when they came near. Ashley made sure he was standing near the back by those stables.

Dave told them that the horses had nets filled with hay during the day. 'In the wild, horses eat little and often,' he said. 'So the hay nets give them something to chew on, and keep them happy. Dry hay gives some horses a cough, though. They have theirs damp. We soak the nets in those water troughs over there. Really heavy to lift they are, when they're wet. And hard to hang up.'

After they had visited the stables he took them into the feed room. He let them run their fingers through the barrels filled with different kinds of food stuffs. 'Coarse mix, chaff, sugar beet. They all have their own special mixtures,' explained Dave.

'I thought horses ate apples and carrots,' said Daniel.

'So they do,' laughed Dave. 'Especially if you want to give them a treat. Most horses rather fancy a peppermint too, but it wouldn't fill them up for long.'

Dave even took them to the muck heap, and they watched some more of the helpers emptying the wheelbarrows onto the heap.

Ashley wrinkled up his nose. 'What happens to it all?' he asked.

'We use the tractor and trailer to move it,' Dave said. 'Gardeners are always glad of the manure! There's a lot of hard, dirty work in a stables, but I wouldn't change my job for anything. Come and look at our rosettes.'

He took them into another shed, where one wall was covered with rosettes, circles of coloured ribbon in blue, red, yellow, mauve, orange, pink and green. They were pinned up in straight rows.

'It looks like Aunt Beth's flower bed,' Ashley whispered to Daniel.

'Those are prizes that our horses have won,' Dave said proudly. 'For jumping, showing, cross-country, dressage.' He saw Ashley looking puzzled. 'They are all different things we train our horses to do,' he explained. 'Anyway, enough facts for now. Time you came and met some of the horses properly.'

Ashley trailed along behind as Dave walked briskly to one of the stables and opened the door. Inside there was a black and white horse standing quietly with her head hanging down.

'This one's Magpie,' he said. 'She's quite old now and really kind. She still does a lot of work. Come round the side of her. Horses can't see you properly if you come straight up from the front. They get frightened of you.'

THEY get frightened! thought Ashley, but he didn't say anything.

Dave showed Daniel how to hold a piece of carrot flat on the palm of his hand, while the old horse snuffled at it and then scooped it up with her rubbery lips. Daniel had a big grin on his face as he wiped his hand down his jeans. Ashley shook his head when he was offered a

turn and lagged rather miserably behind the others as Dave opened the doors and introduced them to what seemed like an endless row of horses.

There were tall ones, with their heads craning on long, stretchy necks over the top of the stable doors. There were short stubby ponies, with the hair from their manes falling into their eyes. There were brown ones and black ones, white ones and spotted ones. Dave taught them the special names for the different colours, dark bay, piebald, strawberry roan.

Why can't they use ordinary words? Ashley thought crossly to himself, as he watched Daniel give yet another piece of carrot. Kangaroo Daniel was really enjoying himself, going up confidently to each new horse. He had a dirty stain down the side of his jeans where he kept wiping his hands, after the carrots.

Dave was stroking the nose of a spotless white horse, which he'd told Daniel and Ashley was really called grey not white.

There we go again, thought Ashley. Silly names.

'Grey horses are always difficult to keep looking good,' said Dave. 'This fellow comes up beautifully after a bath, but you should see him when he's been rolling in the mud!'

Ashley bent down to stroke Ben, the properly grey stable cat which had been following them around. Daniel's really happy, he thought. I wish I was. I didn't realise horses were so complicated and different and big.

Dave smiled at him. 'One more thing,' he said. 'I've saved the best for last.'

He took them to yet another stable and opened the door. Ashley tried to hang back but

Dave took hold of his arm and pulled him forward, so he could see inside. A brown horse was standing right at the back of the stable. Lying on the floor, closer to Ashley, with long legs, brown body and big eyes, was her baby.

As Ashley watched, the foal struggled to its feet. Its legs seemed even longer, and hardly strong enough to hold it up. It looked at Ashley from under long eyelashes and then moved shakily towards its mother. The foal tucked its

head under her belly and its short brushy tail turned round and round as it found the milk it wanted.

'He's beautiful,' said Ashley quietly. 'So small. Can I feed him?'

Dave smiled. 'I thought you'd like him,' he said. 'He's too young for you to feed. But you can give his mother a sugar lump.'

Dave called the horse over and Ashley held out his hand firm and flat with the sugar lump in the middle. He kept his hand still as she snuffled at the sugar, and then carefully picked it up. Ashley felt her warm breath between his fingers.

Suddenly he wanted the moment to last for ever. The quiet darkness of the stable, the leggy foal, his hand damp and warm from the horse's touch.

'I like it here,' he said happily. 'I like horses.'

Chapter 4

'You've not stopped talking horses since the moment you got in.' Aunt Beth laughed. She was sitting on the end of Ashley's bed and they were waiting for Daniel to finish in the bathroom.

She had been cross when they had first got back and she had seen the mud on Daniel's jeans. Kangaroo Daniel had been sent to change, and the jeans had gone straight in the washing machine. She had made them both scrub their hands and use the nailbrush before supper, checking under their finger nails very carefully when they had finished.

'Just like a dinner lady,' Daniel had whispered to Ashley.

But then she had listened patiently as they both talked their way non-stop through the sausage supper. Now it was bedtime and they still hadn't run out of things to say about horses.

'I didn't even like horses this morning,' Ashley was saying, when Daniel, looking very pink and clean, came back into the room. 'But they are brilliant. They are all so different. And that foal is the best of all.'

'You think that because you know a bit more about them,' said Aunt Beth. 'When you don't know much about things, you think they're all the same, just a lot of horses, or fish, or flowers, or even people. But God's world is brilliant. He never runs out of ideas. When we look closely we see how special everything is. Everything he has made is different and special.'

'I know what you mean about people,' said Ashley. 'We can all look the same, especially in a large crowd. But Mum says the same as you. We're all different. She used a funny word. "U" something.'

'Unique,' said Aunt Beth. 'It means just what you said, different and special, and only one of us. Only one Ashley, only one Daniel.'

'And only one Aunt Beth,' finished Daniel.

'You're quite right,' laughed Aunt Beth. 'God is a wonderful maker, and we have to look after everything he has made, especially people, because all people are very special to him.'

'Well I want to do some more looking after of horses,' said Daniel. 'Dave said we can help tomorrow, as well as just watch. We can go back, can't we?'

'Of course you can,' said Aunt Beth. 'As long as he's happy to have you.'

By the middle of the next day Ashley knew he had grown braver. He was still careful to walk in a large circle around the tied up horses, and he wouldn't go into a stable to fill up a water bucket unless the horse was outside, but Dave had let the boys do all sorts of jobs for him, and Ashley was feeling very pleased with himself.

They had helped muck out some of the stables, using a heavy fork and the wheelbarrow. They had carried feed bowls and water buckets to the ponies. Some of the water buckets had been so heavy it had taken the two of them to carry them. Somehow it was always Ashley's legs that got wet, as Kangaroo Daniel bounced along, tipping and wobbling the bucket from his side.

Dave had shown them how to tie the special knots used in the stable for the hay nets and the horses. They were really firm, but a quick pull on one end made the whole thing come undone. Daniel was all fingers and thumbs, and however hard he pulled on his loose end of

rope, all he got was a tangle. He spent a long time practising by himself, and although Vicky kept walking by, she never offered to help him.

'Everyone's nice down there,' he said to Ashley, 'except Vicky. She doesn't seem to want us at all.'

'Time to put all those knots into practice,' Dave said, coming up to them. 'You could get some of the wet hay nets out of the trough and hang them up. They're heavy though. You'll need some muscle!'

Daniel ran over to the trough where the hay was soaking. Some of it was sticking out above the water, and was still dry. Daniel knew what to do. He put his leg into the trough and pressed down hard with his foot. His leg went straight down and the water swirled into the top of his boot.

'I pushed too hard,' he shouted to Ashley, taking his boot off and holding it upside-down so a stream of water came out.

'Don't worry,' called Dave. 'You'll be even wetter when you've finished.'

Ashley and Daniel worked together to lift the heavy hay net out of the water. They carried it between them to the first stable, leaving a trail of drips as they walked. When they got there they put the net on the ground and threaded its string through the tying ring on the wall. With Ashley lifting from underneath and Daniel pulling on the string, they managed to get it fixed into place, although Ashley's front ended up as wet as Daniel's foot.

'We'll change places next time,' he said. 'You push, and I'll pull.'

By the time they reached the last hay net, they were a lot quicker and a lot wetter.

'Easy this, isn't it?' Daniel said, as he threaded the orange-coloured string through the ring and started to pull. 'We must be getting those muscles.' The next second he was lying flat on his back on the straw of the stable. The hay net was still firmly on the ground and the snapped end of the string was in his hand.

'It didn't hurt.' He laughed. 'It's really soft. Great for judo falls!'

He flung himself onto the floor again, rolling over and over, so the straw stuck in his

T-shirt and in his hair.

'It's good for wrestling too,' he said, pulling Ashley down on top of him.

From the next stable Vicky heard them laughing. 'Have you finished yet?' she shouted. 'If you can't do it properly, leave it to me.'

Ashley and Daniel sat up. If there was one thing they didn't like about the stables, it was Vicky.

'She just thinks it's her place and nobody else's,' grumbled Ashley.

'Don't bother about her,' replied Daniel, pulling the straw out of his hair. 'Let's go and look at the ponies, and leave Miss Bossy Boots to it.'

There was one of the ponies that Ashley really liked. He was the smallest of them all. Dave had said he was used for the very small children. He was kept in an open stable, with only a bar across the front, not a door. His name was Sparkie and he was one of the grey-white ones, with a long tangled mane that almost hid his eyes, and a long tangled tail that almost brushed the floor. Ashley felt quite brave about giving him peppermints. The two boys stood for a while watching him.

'Dave said he's got a mind of his own,' said Ashley. 'He's been a riding school pony for so long, he knows just what to do. That's why he's good with small children.'

'I wonder if we'll ever get to ride?' said Daniel. 'We'd need something bigger than Sparkie.'

'Hanging around again!' Vicky pushed past them crossly. 'Come on, that pony's needed for a lesson. If you can't do anything useful, why don't you go home?'

'Are we really in the way?' asked Ashley, when Vicky had gone.

'No,' said Daniel. 'Dave likes us here. Let's go and ask him what we should do next.'

Chapter 5

'I wish I was at the stables and not here,' Ashley thought the next day.

He was standing at the front of the church where Aunt Beth always went on a Sunday. His arms were up in the air and his fingers were spread out like leaves. The vicar, Mr. Roberts, was using the children to help him tell a story from the Bible.

'I want some trees,' he had said, pointing at Ashley and two other children. Daniel had sat safe in his seat, grinning as Ashley had slowly got up and gone to the front of the church.

'There were a lot of trees in this town,' Mr. Roberts went on. 'Palm trees, with tall straight trunks, and fig trees, with really big leaves.'

Ashley spread his fingers even wider.

'The town with all the trees was in the land where Jesus lived,' Mr. Roberts said. 'The town was called Jericho. A lot of the people who lived in Jericho were really excited because Jesus was going to come to their town. They'd heard all sorts of things about him. They wanted to see him for themselves. So they left their houses and came out to watch in the street, in front of the trees.'

He lined up some chairs by Ashley and the other children. 'Houses,' he said. 'White and square. And now we need a big crowd of people.'

He called some more children to the front.

'There aren't enough of you,' he said, 'so you'll have to look big! Some of the crowd were already with Jesus. They'd been there when Jesus had spoken to a blind man just outside town. And now the blind man was walking with them. Jesus had made him able to see. The big crowd of people, with Jesus in the middle, came into the town. Even more people came to join them. So pretend that you are part of the crowd of people, all around

Jesus, all packed together in the hot sun. Can you keep up with him? Can you see? Will Jesus stop and talk to you?

'Then someone else came looking for Jesus. This man was a bit late. He came by himself. He saw the crowd, but he couldn't see Jesus, because there were people all around him.'

Mr. Roberts took hold of Daniel's hand and brought him to the front. Now it was Ashley's turn to grin.

'This man was one of the richest men in town. He was only a little man, very small, and very rich. He had no real friends. No-one liked him because he worked for the leaders in the town, who came from another country, and he cheated the townspeople out of their money. They saw him there, but nobody in the crowd made a space for him. The rich man, whose name was Zacchaeus, looked around. He did want to see Jesus, but no-one would let him stand at the front and he was too short to see from the back. Then he saw one of the trees with its big leaves. Secret, shady, and tall. He knew he had found just the place. Soon Jesus and the crowd would be walking past the tree. He'd be able to see from up a tree. He went to the tree, and he climbed into it.'

Mr. Roberts stood Daniel on a chair next to Ashley.

'Now Zacchaeus could see. He didn't care if he looked silly. He just wanted to see Jesus. Jesus came nearer and nearer, and then he did a very strange thing. He walked right past the crowds of people, straight up to the tree where Zacchaeus was hiding in the big leaves. He

stopped in front of it, and told Zacchaeus to
come down. When the people saw who Jesus
was talking to, they started muttering, "What's
he talking to him for? Doesn't he know he's
no good? We don't like him." But Jesus loved
Zacchaeus. After he had come down from the
tree, they went to Zacchaeus' house together
and talked for a long time.'

Mr. Roberts moved Daniel from his chair
and stood beside him.

'Zacchaeus was changed by meeting Jesus,' he said. 'He didn't need to cheat and steal any more. He knew he was special, because Jesus loved him, even though no-one else wanted him.

'Zacchaeus gave back a lot of the money he had stolen, and he started to care about other people. He really was changed. He stayed small, but he didn't stay left out! We need to remember that we are all special to God. God sent Jesus to show us just how special we are, so special that he even died for us.'

'Thank you, trees and people,' he said, turning to the children. 'You've been a great help.'

Ashley wriggled his fingers. It had been hard work keeping them out as leaves all that time.

'That was good fun,' whispered Daniel, as they went back to their seats. 'You make a good tree.'

'I'd rather climb one than be one,' answered Ashley. 'I'm stiff!'

Chapter 6

'Wouldn't you like to do something different today?' Aunt Beth asked at breakfast.

'No,' they said together. 'There aren't any horses at home!'

Aunt Beth laughed. 'I'm just glad you're happy,' she said, 'and Dave says you're useful.'

'It's really good,' said Ashley, 'I like it all. I like the horses. I like the things we do. I like the people down there.'

'Well perhaps not all the people,' Daniel chipped in.

'What do you mean?' asked Aunt Beth.

'There's this one girl,' went on Daniel. 'Vicky. She's a really good rider, but she just won't be friends. I don't think she wants us down there.

I think she thinks we get in the way. Still, everyone else is nice, so it doesn't really matter about her.'

'Oh yes it does,' said Aunt Beth, firmly. 'Everyone matters. Remember the story about Zacchaeus.'

'But she's horrible to us,' said Ashley. 'She was cross when Daniel fell over, and she doesn't help us when we get stuck.'

'Well you just think about it,' said Aunt Beth. 'Jesus said everyone is special, not just the people you happen to like. Off you go now, but don't forget about Zacchaeus' story. It might make a difference to the way you get on with Vicky.'

They walked slowly down the track from the lane to the stable yard. The ground was bumpy where the tractor had driven over it, but the sun had dried the mud hard. Kangaroo Daniel hopped from ridge to ridge, giving an especially large bounce over a pile of droppings.

'They're soft,' he said. 'Horses have been this way already!'

54

'So you're a detective now, are you?' laughed Ashley.

At the end of the path was a large gate which was usually kept closed. Today it was open, and Vicky was leaning against the post.

'Hi, Vicky,' called Ashley clearly.

Daniel looked at him sharply.

'It doesn't hurt to say hello,' said Ashley.

When she saw them Vicky walked towards them. 'You're in trouble today,' she said crossly,

ignoring Ashley's hello. 'You're always fussing around Sparkie. It must have been you who left his bolt undone. He's got out and run away. You just wait till Dave sees you. He's really cross.'

'We've only just got here,' said Daniel firmly. 'And we weren't here at all yesterday. Whatever it is, it's not our fault.'

'That's not what Dave thinks,' Vicky said.

When they found Dave he was looking very worried, but he wasn't cross with Ashley and Daniel. That morning he had taken Sparkie his feed as usual. He had found the stable empty. The little pony was missing.

'The worst thing would be if he'd got up on to the road,' he said. 'I don't think anyone would steal him, but you never know. We need to search, fast.'

Dave asked Daniel and Ashley to look in the closest fields, just behind the stables. He and some of the others went up to the main road. Daniel waited until Dave and the others had gone out of sight, and then he pulled at Ashley's arm.

'Let's go the other way. Remember those droppings. I'm sure he's gone that way.'

'We ought to do what Dave said,' Ashley began, but Daniel had already run off. When Ashley caught up with him he was down on his knees, peering through the thick hedge beside the path. He was pulling at the brambles with his hands, trying to make a hole large enough to see through.

'I'm sure he's in there,' he said over his shoulder to Ashley. 'I can see something moving.' He began snapping off some of the twigs right at the bottom of the hedge, where there was a bit of a hollow, and before Ashley could stop him, was wriggling through on his

57

tummy. Ashley looked through the hedge himself. He saw Daniel scramble to his feet, inside the field.

'It was only an empty plastic bag,' he called crossly, picking up the bag and waving it at Ashley. 'Perhaps Sparkie is in the next field,' he said. He took off at a run across the tufty grass.

Ashley sighed. He didn't know whether to stay or follow. He looked through the gap again and could just see Daniel scrambling over the fence at the far side of the field. Vicky came up silently behind him. 'What are you doing here?' she asked. 'This isn't where Dave told you to look.'

Ashley told her about Daniel, and what he thought he had seen.

'We can't leave him,' Vicky said crossly. 'We'd better go and look for him together.'

Vicky was a fast runner, and Ashley was quite out of breath by the time he caught up with her at the far fence.

'They're both in that field,' she said excitedly. 'But that silly boy's running after Sparkie and getting him in a panic. He'll never catch him that way.'

Ashley looked where Vicky was pointing. Kangaroo Daniel was chasing Sparkie. They could see him waving his arms up and down, and they could hear him shouting. Sparkie and Kangaroo Daniel were both running in circles round the field. Sometimes the pony would stand still, so Daniel almost caught up with

him. Just when Daniel reached out for him, the little pony would toss his head and gallop off again, leaving Daniel behind.

'I can catch him,' Vicky said.

She called to Daniel, and made him stand still. Then she moved slowly towards Sparkie who had stopped running and was peacefully chewing at the grass. As she got close the little pony lifted his head, stared at her from under his long fringe, and then trotted briskly away.

'She'll never catch him,' Ashley said out loud.

Vicky put her hand in her pocket and, standing still, began talking softly to Sparkie. To Ashley's surprise the pony stopped and looked. He started moving steadily towards her, until she was close enough to grasp a thick handful of mane, and throw a rope over his neck. The pony snuffled at her pocket. Vicky gently put his head collar on and Sparkie followed calmly behind her as she led him towards the boys.

'That was brilliant,' said Daniel, running up, puffing. 'He wouldn't stop for me. How did you do it?'

Vicky took an empty crisp packet out of her pocket.

'It's a good trick,' she said. 'He heard me rustle that, and he thought it was food. He's a greedy little thing. It was clever of you to see the droppings in the lane, though. Dave will be pleased that he's safe.'

'You were brilliant to catch him like that,' Daniel said again.

They all helped to put Sparkie safely back where he belonged and made sure the bolt was firmly closed. Dave took them into the rosette shed and gave them a drink of orange juice to celebrate.

Ashley sat day-dreaming as Vicky and Daniel told Dave what had happened. It was nice to have Vicky being friendly to them at last. Maybe she wouldn't mind them helping at the stables now. He looked happily round the shed, over at the wall of rosettes. He was beginning to feel really at home here. Then he looked sharply back at the wall again. There were some gaps in the bottom row, where two or three of the rosettes were missing. Ashley was sure it hadn't been like that before.

'What's happened to the rosettes?' he asked, interrupting the others.

They turned round to see and Dave stood up to look.

'I expect they have got knocked down,' Vicky said sharply. 'Don't fuss. I'm going to get on. There's lots to do.'

She put her drink down on the table and walked out of the shed.

Chapter 7

'I hate getting changed,' said Daniel with disgust, as he wriggled a clean T-shirt over his head.

'We can't go out for tea in our stable clothes,' Ashley said. 'They smell. It won't be too bad. I want to see those new kittens.'

A friend of Aunt Beth's had invited her and the boys out to tea, to see some new kittens she had in the house. At first they'd felt a bit grumbly. They didn't want to be clean and tidy. But when they got to the house they found that Aunt Beth's friend, whose name was Gill, was a friendly, chatty person. She soon had them settled down with drinks and a plate of chocolate biscuits.

'You get to know these little chaps, while your aunt and I have a good chat,' she said, bringing in a cardboard box and putting it down in front of them.

Ashley and Daniel knelt by the box, looking into it. There were three kittens in it, all different, one grey, one tabby, one black. Two of them lay snuggled up in one corner, their legs and tails curled round each other. The tabby one was standing on his legs, scratching at the side of the box. He was mewing noisily, and Ashley could see a row of tiny but sharp teeth.

'You can pick him up,' said Gill. 'Use both hands and don't squeeze.'

Ashley held the warm, slender, tabby body in his cupped hands. The kitten opened his blue eyes wide and stared solemnly at him.

'He's beautiful,' he said. 'What are you going to do with him?'

'We can't keep him,' said Gill. 'We've already got two other cats. Find a good home I suppose.'

'Where are your girls today?' asked Aunt Beth.

Ashley stroked the kitten with his finger while he listened to Gill talking about her daughters. Two of them were away at a gymnastics competition. They spent a lot of time with a gym club. Gill pointed to a whole row of silver cups and medals on a shelf in a cupboard. 'They do really well,' she said. 'They've won a lot of things.'

'Those are horse rosettes,' said Ashley, looking at another shelf.

'Yes,' said Gill proudly. 'That's my youngest daughter. They're the first she's ever won.'

Daniel put out his hands to take the kitten from Ashley.

'My turn now,' he said.

Ashley carefully undid the kitten's sharp claws from his T-shirt and put him gently into Kangaroo Daniel's cupped hands. Almost immediately Daniel flung the kitten back in the box. He looked at his hands and started wiping them down his jeans.

'Ugh! He's made me all wet,' he said with disgust.

'Go and wash your hands properly,' said Aunt Beth. 'His mum will teach him how to use a litter tray soon.'

Ashley laughed. Trust Kangaroo Daniel. The kitten had sat so calmly with him. He looked round as Daniel came back into the room. Just as he pushed the door closed, it opened again, and a girl followed him in.

'This is Vicky, my youngest daughter,' said Gill.

Ashley and Daniel looked up together. There was no mistaking her. Long ginger hair and dirty jodhpurs!

'I didn't know this was Vicky's house,' whispered Daniel.

Ashley didn't answer. He looked at the rosettes in the corner of the room, thinking hard. Gill was busy getting more biscuits and making another pot of tea, talking away to Aunt Beth as she worked. He looked at Vicky.

'Those are the rosettes from the stable, aren't they?' he said.

'Don't say anything here, please,' Vicky whispered. 'I'll tell you later.'

They didn't have a chance to talk to Vicky until later the next day. Aunt Beth took them out in the car in the morning. It was lunchtime when they got to the stables. They settled themselves in the rosette room, with packets of crisps and a thick cheese sandwich each. Vicky came in, munching an apple. 'You stole those rosettes,' said Daniel fiercely. 'You're just a cheat. I don't want to be friends with you.'

'I didn't think of it as stealing,' said Vicky slowly. 'I took them to make things better at home. You don't know what it's really like there. My sisters are good at everything. Every time they go to gym they bring a prize home. Mum goes on and on about it. You've seen the shelf.'

Ashley nodded.

'Well I'm not really like that,' Vicky went on. 'I'm not especially good at anything. I've never won anything. Mum would be so pleased if I brought a medal home and she could show it off. So I thought about the rosettes. It was quite safe really. Mum never comes down here. She wouldn't know I hadn't really won them. Dave is Dad's friend, and Dad doesn't live at home any more, so they'd never find out. And Mum was pleased. She cleared the shelf especially for them.'

'It's cheating,' said Daniel firmly. 'And stealing. You shouldn't have done it.'

He stood up, scattering bits of cheese to the floor. 'Come on, Ashley. We don't want to sit around here,' he said.

Ashley was thinking hard. Cheating. Yes it

was. Just like that other cheat, Zacchaeus. No-
one had liked him. But Jesus had gone straight
to him. He looked at Vicky. It must be hard to
feel left out. Not to know you were special.
Perhaps that was why she had been so mean
to them all the time, because they were taking
her special place at the stables. He suddenly
felt sorry for her. She needed to be sure she was
special too. He made up his mind, and held
out his packet of crisps.

'Have some,' he said, 'Salt and vinegar. We won't say anything, but you ought to put them back.'

Vicky smiled and took a handful of crisps. Daniel began to splutter crossly. Ashley whispered to him, 'Remember Zacchaeus!' Before Daniel could say anything else, Dave stuck his head round the door.

'That little pickle, Sparkie, has run away again,' he said.

Chapter 8

They ran with Dave to Sparkie's stable, and just as Dave had said, Sparkie was gone. The ponies on either side stood drowsily still, but Sparkie's bar was pushed back and his space was empty.

'I don't know what's going on,' Dave said, 'but at least we know where to look for him. We'll try that field where you found him last time.'

Daniel raced off to the field where they had found Sparkie before. Ashley and Vicky went after him. Dave went off with some of the other helpers. But it wasn't long before they were all back together in the yard. No-one had found Sparkie. He was still missing. Dave was looking more worried.

'I'm afraid he might have wandered out into the lane this time,' he said. 'Or even the road. We'll have to keep looking. Perhaps you three could walk along the lane to your aunt's house, and we'll go the other way.'

On any other morning, Ashley would have enjoyed the walk back down to his aunt's bungalow, but now they were all anxious. Kangaroo Daniel was zigzagging across the lane, jumping up to see over the hedges of the fields.

'Sheep and cows,' he said, 'plenty of them. But I can't see Sparkie.'

'I hope he hasn't got out onto the main road,' said Vicky. 'That would be awful.'

'What are we going to do now?' Ashley asked, as they reached Aunt Beth's bungalow and the end of the lane.

'Go back, I suppose,' said Vicky sadly. 'We could walk on the house side this time.'

The few houses between Aunt Beth's and the stable lane all had large gardens. Some of the hedges were very high and Daniel went a little way down each driveway. Once he started

a dog barking, but otherwise everything seemed peaceful and still. There was no sign at all of the little grey pony, with a tangled mane over its eyes and a long tangled tail trailing to the ground.

'Suppose he's hurt,' said Ashley. 'I couldn't bear it.'

'There's someone,' said Daniel, nudging Ashley. 'Let's ask if he's seen anything.'

There was a man working in the front garden of the next house. He was piling grass cuttings into a big wheelbarrow. He looked up and frowned when he saw the children, but answered straight away when he heard what they wanted. It was no use. He'd only just come out into the front garden, and hadn't seen anything.

'It's always quiet round here,' he said.

Then they heard a woman shout, 'Get away from here! Get out, you nasty thing!'

There was a loud scream.

Kangaroo Daniel turned and raced down the lane. Ashley and Vicky followed him. They found him waiting for them by the gate of a house further up the lane.

'I didn't chase him this time,' he said. 'But he's there. Come and see.'

He led them down the open sideway to the back of the house.

They saw a beautiful striped green lawn. In the middle of it a woman was standing waving a pillowslip up and down.

'Is it yours?' she shouted. 'Make it go away. See what it's done!'

The three children looked round. The flowers in the flower bed were squashed and broken. There were hoof prints all over the smooth grass. A basket of washing lay on its side with clothes spilling out of it. There were T-shirts and socks lying on the ground. Sparkie was standing still under a round washing line, a pink sheet tangled over his back and around his legs.

'Get it out,' shrieked the woman again, flapping the pillowslip in her hand. 'Look at my washing! Look what that animal's done to my garden!'

Sparkie moved sharply backwards and rolled his eyes, pulling on the sheet. His ears were flat against his head.

'Don't do that,' said Vicky. 'You'll frighten him even more. I'll get him. He's caught up in all those clothes.'

She moved slowly towards Sparkie, talking gently as she went. He pawed at the ground with his front foot, treading the sheet into the grass. He couldn't move away. Vicky went right up to him. She slipped a rope round his neck.

Daniel gave a loud cheer, and the woman glared at him.

'He's all tangled up,' said Vicky softly, bending down and unwrapping the pink sheet from Sparkie's leg. 'It's a good job it's only washing and not wire.'

The woman. didn't look at all pleased as Vicky led Sparkie towards her.

'I'm sorry about your washing,' Vicky said, before she could say anything. 'As soon as we've got Sparkie back we'll ask Dave to come round and see you. Come on you two!'

She made Sparkie trot and they went quickly back to the lane.

'Pink sheets! Wrapped up in a washing line! What will he get up to next?'

Once Sparkie had been safely put away and the bar bolted, Dave listened to their story with amazement. Daniel told him about the woman flapping the pillowslip up and down. He waved his arms about and made his voice high and squeaky, like hers had been. Dave laughed.

'I wish I'd seen it,' he said. 'I'd better get round there to try and put things right. New sheets at least, I expect.'

'Vicky was great,' said Daniel. 'She knew just what to do.'

Vicky looked pleased, and she smiled back at Daniel.

'You're not getting so bad around horses yourself,' she said. 'I'll give you a ride on my horse, April, tomorrow, if that's all right with Dave.'

Dave nodded and Daniel beamed. Ashley looked thoughtful. Horses from the ground were all right now. Horses when you were up on their back? Well he wasn't so sure.

Suddenly he stumbled forward, bumping into Dave. 'Don't push me, Daniel,' Ashley said. 'If you can ride, so can I.'

'I didn't push you,' said Daniel excitedly. 'Look behind you.'

Ashley turned his head. Sparkie was standing right behind him. The little pony pushed at Ashley again, sending him wobbling forward.

'Sparkie!' spluttered Ashley. 'But I thought we'd shut him in!'

Sparkie nuzzled his head against Ashley and stood quietly. Dave ran off to the stable and

came back with a smile on his face.

'Now I understand,' he said. 'Come and see.'

He led Sparkie back to his stall and pulled the bar across, bolting it firmly.

'I knew some horses could do this,' he said. 'I just didn't know Sparkie was one of them. Watch.'

Sparkie put his head down and drank noisily from his water bucket. He stood looking at them from under his fringe, the water dripping from his lips. Then he bent his head down and put his teeth firmly round the bar of the bolt. He shook his head and pulled, and the bolt slid smoothly out of its hole. He moved forward against the bar and pushed it open.

'He's learnt a new trick,' said Dave. 'Now I've got two jobs to do. I've got to buy a new set of sheets. And I've got to find a way to stop Sparkie running away again.'

Chapter 9

Vicky kept her promise. When the boys arrived at the stable the next day she had her horse ready, waiting for them. April was black all over, apart from a white fish-shaped mark on her side. She was wearing the red cloth under her saddle, and her velvety coat was shining in the sun.

'Dave says we can get started straight away,' she said. 'You'll need to get hats from the shed. He'll help you fit them.'

She led April into the sandy area.

Ashley felt silly in his riding hat. He stood and watched as Vicky showed Kangaroo Daniel how to get up on the horse. He knew he was nervous. Wheelbarrows and hay nets, water buckets and sweeping. That was all right. He knew he liked being around horses. He just wasn't sure he wanted to ride one. Daniel sat up very straight as Vicky showed him where to put his legs and how to hold the reins.

'You're quite safe. Just feel her move,' she said, as she started to walk April round.

'Those painted letters tell you where to go,' she went on. 'We'll start at "A" and walk straight down the middle to "C." '

'We wondered what they spelt when we first watched you,' said Daniel.

'They don't spell anything. They are just markers.' Vicky answered. 'There's an easy way to remember them though. It's the first letters of a sentence. All King Edward's Horses Canter Madly Before Fighting.'

'I like that,' said Daniel, and he said it over in his head, as Vicky led him round the school, past the letters.

All King Edward's Horses Canter Madly Before Fighting.

He said it again, faster.

'All King Edward's Horses Canter Madly Before Fighting.'

'When can I go faster?' he asked.

Vicky laughed. 'I'll make her trot if you like,' she said. 'You'll find it bumpy. Just let yourself go up and down, and hold on to the front of the saddle if you think you are slipping.'

Vicky started to run, and Daniel found himself bumping up and down as April began to trot.

'That was great,' he said, a bit out of breath,

when they stopped again. 'Now can I do it by myself?'

'I'll let go for a minute and walk beside you,' she said.

Daniel squeezed with his legs and April started to walk slowly forward. It wasn't fast enough for Kangaroo Daniel. Letting go of the rein with one hand, he slapped hard on April's side. She shot forward. Daniel lost his balance. He slipped sideways and landed on the ground with a bump. He stood up quickly with a very red face.

'I'm all right,' he said. 'Let's have another go.'

This time Daniel stayed on until his turn was over.

'I don't know how you make it look so easy,' he said, when he was back on the ground. 'Ashley and I watched you over the fence on our first day. You were jumping really well.'

'I'm lucky I can get here so often,' Vicky said.

'You're good enough to win a rosette of your own one day,' smiled Ashley.

'Perhaps I will,' said Vicky, grinning at him. 'That's what Dave said when I told him what I'd done with the other rosettes. Come on Ashley. Your turn now.'

Ashley was quite sure he didn't want to land on the ground like Kangaroo Daniel. He listened carefully to Vicky and made sure she kept close to him. He found he was quite enjoying it, the smooth movement, the feel of the horse's long mane ruffling over his fingers.

'I'd like to do that again!' he said when they'd finished. 'We go home tomorrow. Do you think we will ever come back?'

'I know you will,' said Vicky. 'Sooner than you think. Mum and your Aunt Beth have arranged for you to have one of our kittens each. You're coming round this afternoon to choose. And you'll be coming back in three weeks to collect them, when they are ready to leave their mother.'

Ashley and Daniel spent a long time looking at the kittens. Daniel knew he didn't want the tabby one.

'Not after what he did to me,' he said. 'I don't want any more puddles!'

Ashley wasn't sure. He liked the tabby one, but it was the smallest now, and he knew you were supposed to choose a big, strong kitten. The grey one had short, thick fur. It was very pretty. But he remembered how the tabby one had sat so still in his hands, and the way its small claws had hooked into his T-shirt. He would like to look after that one.

Kangaroo Daniel made up his mind. 'I'd like the black one,' he said. 'I want to call it April, because it's the same colour as Vicky's horse.'

'Perhaps you can teach her to jump, then,' laughed Vicky. 'Only don't fall off!'

Ashley sat and looked a bit longer. What a lot had happened since they came to Aunt Beth's. What a lot he would have to tell his mum. He hadn't wanted her to leave him. Now he and Kangaroo Daniel were friends with Vicky and liked horses so much that Daniel had called his kitten after one. Suddenly he knew he had no choice. There was only one kitten he could have, a special one for him. He picked up the tabby one again.

'I'd like this one,' he said, 'because he's small, and because he's special to me. I'm going to call him Zac, short for Zacchaeus. Look after him for me, Vicky, until it's time to take him home.'

'Of course I will,' she said. 'And you can both have another riding lesson when you come to collect them.'

'That'll be great!' Daniel and Ashley said at the same time, 'Just great!'

Other titles in the Read by Myself series

Kangaroo Daniel and the Canal Holiday

Dilys Gower

Ashley wasn't sure he'd heard properly. Take Daniel on holiday with them! Kangaroo Daniel in *his* cabin, sleeping in one of *his* bunk beds, bouncing all over everywhere.

He opened his mouth to say 'No!' as loudly as he could but Mum was not waiting to hear what he thought.

Kangaroo Daniel usually causes disasters wherever he goes but on the canal holiday he ends up rescuing Ashley.

Amy T and Grandma B

Eileen Taylor

Amy T hung on to Matthew's jumper as he rushed across the huge showroom.

'Here it is,' he said.

Amy T walked round a very large box which was open at the top. Inside were hundreds of light, hollow balls. 'Come on! Climb in!' said Matthew, who was already diving amongst the balls.

All sorts of fun things happen when Amy T and Matthew visit Grandma B.

The Other Kitten

Patricia St John

Mark and Carol are enjoying a spring holiday at Gran's house by the seaside. One day they see a notice on a gate, offering free kittens and go to investigate.

Mark picked up a black kitten with four white paws and a white nose. 'We'll have this one,' he said.

'No,' said Carol, picking up a grey tabby, 'we're having this one, and I'll call it Fluff because it's so soft.' Mark and Carol's quarrel over choosing a kitten nearly ends in disaster.

Friska my Friend

Patricia St John

When Colin discovers the hungry dog left at the empty cottage he persuades his parents to let him keep her while her owner is in hospital.

Colin ran to the house. The dog came barking to greet him – he flung his arms round her neck. 'You're mine and I'm going to call you Friska,' he whispered.

Colin's special friendship with Friska helps him to understand what 'you are mine' really means.